JACK

Based on *The Railway Series* by the Rev. W. Awdry

Illustrations by
Robin Davies and Jerry Smith

EGMONT

EGMONT

We bring stories to life

First published in Great Britain 2006
by Egmont UK Limited
239 Kensington High Street, London W8 6SA

Thomas the Tank Engine & Friends™

A BRITT ALLCROFT COMPANY PRODUCTION

Based on The Railway Series by The Reverend W Awdry
© 2006 Gullane (Thomas) LLC. A HIT Entertainment Company

Thomas the Tank Engine & Friends and Thomas & Friends are trademarks of Gullane Entertainment Inc.
Thomas the Tank Engine & Friends is Reg. U.S. Pat. & Tm. Off.

ISBN 978 1 4052 2365 2
ISBN 1 4052 2365 0
3 5 7 9 10 8 6 4
Printed in Great Britain

This is a story about Jack the Front Loader. When he came to the Island of Sodor, he couldn't wait to get to work at the Quarry. But rushing in too quickly got him into trouble with the rest of The Pack …

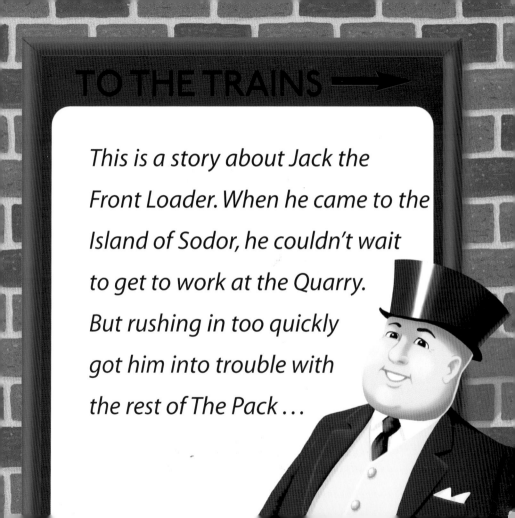

It was a tingly spring morning on the Island of Sodor. Thomas was excited. The Fat Controller had sent him to collect a new Special from Jenny Packard.

Miss Jenny ran the yard where all the diggers, cranes and lorries on Sodor lived.

At the yard, Jack was waiting for Thomas.

I'm Jack the Front Loader," he whirred, proudly. "I can load … and unload … and carry lots of things."

"I can haul and shunt," boasted Thomas.

Thomas and Jack set off for the Quarry.

"Is this your first job at the Quarry?"
called Thomas.

"It's my first job on the Island," Jack called back.
"I can't wait to get to work!"

At the Quarry, The Pack was working hard. Jack wanted to say "hello" to everyone, but they were all too busy to stop and talk.

He scooted towards Oliver, the big excavator. "I'm Jack. Can I help?" he asked.

"Oh, no," Oliver replied. "Help Byron."

Byron the Bulldozer was shoving rock and rubble with his giant blade.

"I'm Jack. Can I help?" asked Jack.

"I don't need help," boomed Byron busily. "Try Kelly the Crane."

"I'm Jack!" Jack whirred, rushing up to Kelly the crane.

"Mind my paint!" snapped a lorry. "You should watch where you're going!"

"Isobella!" scolded Kelly.

"Sorry," said Isobella sourly. "But it's too busy here for rushing and pushing."

"The Quarry can be dangerous," Kelly told Jack. "Safety first! Why don't you go and help Alfie?"

"I'm sorry," said Jack. "I'll try to be more careful."

Jack found Alfie the Excavator digging a big hole. "I'm Jack," he said. "Can I help you with your work?"

Alfie gave him a big smile. "More help means more dirt. More dirt means more fun! I'm Alfie," he replied.

Jack and Alfie were soon working hard and having lots of fun.

But Jack was worried that the other machines didn't like him. He wished he could really be part of The Pack.

The next day, Thomas chuffed along the branch line, thinking about his new friend, Jack.

Thomas couldn't wait to get to the Old Quarry Bridge. He knew The Pack were working there.

He could see how Jack was doing. "I hope he's settling in," puffed Thomas.

At the bridge, Jack and Alfie were loading the dump truck, Max. Dust and dirt were flying everywhere. Work had never been such fun!

Jack felt very proud. He had tried hard and been very careful. He hoped The Pack would see what a good worker he was and Miss Jenny would let him stay.

Later that day, Ned the Steam Shovel was moving under the bridge.

"I must be careful my crane arm doesn't hit the bridge," he said to himself.

But Ned hadn't lowered his tall crane arm far enough. It knocked loose the important keystones from the top of the bridge.

The bridge started to crumble … just as Thomas puffed towards it, unaware of the danger ahead!

Jack saw the danger. "Thomas!" he shouted.

Jack jumped in and lifted his front loader up to the bridge. He pushed with all his might.

Thomas saw the Flagman and his Driver applied the brakes but they couldn't stop in time.

"Cinders and ashes!" cried Thomas.

The stones were very heavy, but Jack didn't let go …

Thomas crossed the bridge safely and whooshed to a halt.

"Hold on, Jack!" called Kelly. And he rushed to help.

But Jack couldn't hold on any longer. The bridge came tumbling down.

"Are you all right, Jack?" asked Kelly.

"I think so," he replied.

But his arms were badly bent.

Thomas took Jack back to the yard.

Jack was afraid that Miss Jenny would be cross with him – he had jumped in without thinking about safety, and damaged his arms.

But Miss Jenny was pleased. "Well done, Jack!" she said. "It's off to the fitters with you, tomorrow. The Pack can't have a front loader with bent arms!"

"You mean I can stay?" whirred Jack.

"You're part of the crew," Miss Jenny grinned.

"Welcome to The Pack, Jack!" shouted Alfie.

Kelly and Isobella cheered.

Jack was so happy he couldn't think of anything to say. So he just revved his engine and bounced his bucket.

Thomas was very pleased that his friend could stay. "Welcome to The Pack, Jack," he whistled. "Peep! Peep!"

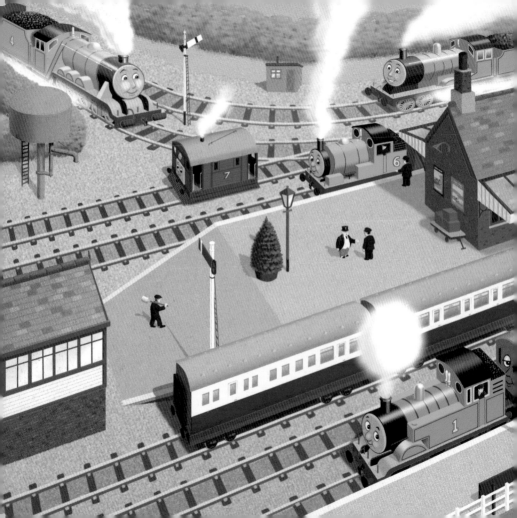

The Thomas Story Library is THE definitive collection of stories about Thomas and ALL his Friends.

5 more Thomas Story Library titles will be chuffing into your local bookshop in April 2007:

Arthur
Caroline
Murdoch
Neville
Freddie

And there are even more
Thomas Story Library books to follow later!
So go on, start your Thomas Story Library NOW!

A Fantastic Offer for Thomas the Tank Engine Fans!

STICK
POUND
COIN
HERE

In every Thomas Story Library book like this one, you will find a special token. Collect 6 Thomas tokens and we will send you a brilliant Thomas poster, and a double-sided bedroom door hanger!
Simply tape a £1 coin in the space above, and fill out the form overleaf.

TO BE COMPLETED BY AN ADULT

To apply for this great offer, ask an adult to complete the coupon below
and send it with a pound coin and 6 tokens, to:
THOMAS OFFERS, PO BOX 715, HORSHAM RH12 5WG

☐ Please send a Thomas poster and door hanger. I enclose 6 tokens
plus a £1 coin. (Price includes P&P)

Fan's name...

Address...

....Postcode..................................

Date of birth...

Name of parent/guardian...

Signature of parent/guardian...